Seven Fables from
AESOP

Retold and illustrated by R.W. Alley

DODD, MEAD & COMPANY • NEW YORK

design by Antler & Baldwin, Inc.

1   2   3   4   5   6   7   8   9   10

Library of Congress Cataloging-in-Publication Data
Alley, R. W. (Robert W.)   Seven fables from Aesop.
Contents: The shepherd boy and the wolf—
The milkmaid and her pail—The fox and the grapes—[etc.]
1. Fables. [1. Fables] I. Title
PZ8.2.A45Se 1986   398.2′452 [E]   86-2025
ISBN 0-396-08820-1

Contents

The Shepherd Boy and the Wolf

There was once a young shepherd boy who grew bored with his work of tending the sheep. He longed for a little excitement. So he decided to play a trick on the people of his village just to stir things up a bit. The shepherd boy shouted out as loudly as he could, "WOLF! WOLF! There's a wolf eating up the sheep!"

In the village, the people heard the boy's "desperate" cries.
They left their work. They picked up sticks. They pulled
up stones. And they ran to the pasture to save the shepherd
boy's flock from the wolf.

But when the villagers got to the pasture, the shepherd boy just laughed and called them names. "You silly people, there is no wolf. It was all a joke, just for fun. I wanted to see how fast all of you could run."

The shepherd boy was quite amused by his trick. However, the villagers did not find it funny. They walked home grumbling and mumbling. They were very angry.

A week went by and the shepherd boy became bored again. He shouted out as loudly as he could, "WOLF! WOLF!

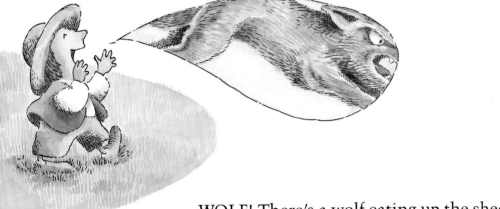

WOLF! There's a wolf eating up the sheep!"

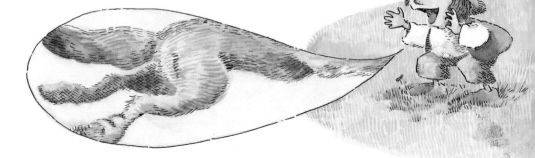

Again, the people from the village came running with their sticks and stones. Again, the shepherd boy laughed at them. And, again, the villagers walked home very angry.

Then, one day, the shepherd boy really did see a wolf run in among the sheep.
The terrified boy shouted out as loudly as he could,
"WOLF! WOLF! There's a wolf eating up the sheep. Help!
Come quickly! WOLF! WOLF!"

But, this time, the people from the village did not come running. They went on with their work. And they left the sticks and stones where they were. The villagers had been tricked by the shepherd boy twice before. They were sure that the boy's cries were nothing but lies.

So the wolf had the last laugh and gobbled up all he could of the flock.

A liar will never be trusted, even when he tells the truth.

The Milkmaid and Her Pail

here was once a milkmaid who loved to daydream about what could be.

One day the milkmaid was coming down a hill carrying a full pail of milk balanced on her head. It was a long walk and so she began to daydream. The milkmaid said to herself:

"The milk in this pail will give me cream.
The cream I will churn into butter.
And the butter I will take to market to sell.

With the money I earn from the butter I will buy eggs.
The eggs will hatch into chicks.
The chicks will grow into fat chickens.
The fat chickens I will take to the market to sell.
With the money I earn from the fat chickens I will buy
a fine dress.

And the dress I will wear to the fair.
At the fair I will catch the eye of a handsome Prince.
The Prince will take my hand.
And I will curtsy ever so gracefully."

Then the milkmaid, lost in her daydream, curtsied right there on the hill. Down fell the pail! All the milk was spilled. And just like the milk, all the milkmaid's dreams and schemes vanished.

Do not count your chickens before they are hatched.

The Fox and the Grapes

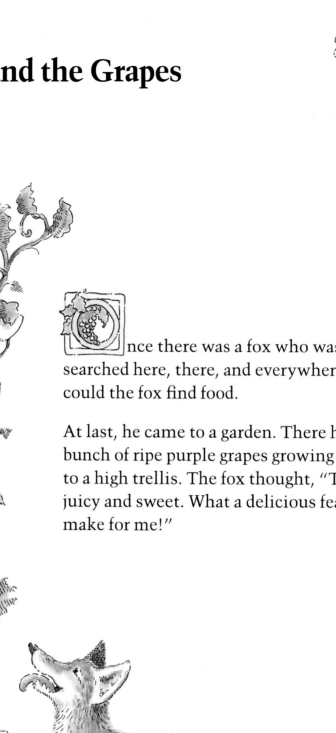

Once there was a fox who was very hungry. He searched here, there, and everywhere, but nowhere could the fox find food.

At last, he came to a garden. There he saw a tempting bunch of ripe purple grapes growing on a vine tied to a high trellis. The fox thought, "Those grapes look so juicy and sweet. What a delicious feast they will make for me!"

The fox jumped up to pull down the grapes. But he didn't jump high enough. He tried again. This time he jumped a little higher, but the grapes were still beyond his grasp. No matter how hard he tried, the fox could not reach the grapes.

Finally, too tired to jump anymore, the fox gave up. "On second look, those grapes are really quite withered and overripe. I am sure they are sour anyway," muttered the fox as he walked out of the garden.

Some pretend to despise what they cannot have.

The Lion and the Mouse

nce a great lion lay asleep in the tall golden grass. Suddenly, a small mouse happened to scamper across the lion's nose. The lion woke up and roared in anger. He seized the mouse by its tail and swung it up to his mouth. The mouse shook with fear. He was sure he would be eaten.

"Please, Mr. Lion, sir," squeaked the small creature, "if you spare my life now, I promise I will repay your kindness some day."

At this, the lion smiled. "How could such a tiny thing as this mouse ever be able to help so great and strong an animal as myself?" thought the lion. But since he was no longer angry, the lion let the little mouse go free.

Not long afterward the great lion was walking through the
thick jungle when he tripped a hunter's trap. A heavy net
fell down around him. The more the lion struggled, the
more firmly he became entangled in the net. The lion feared
he was trapped for good and let out a thunderous roar.

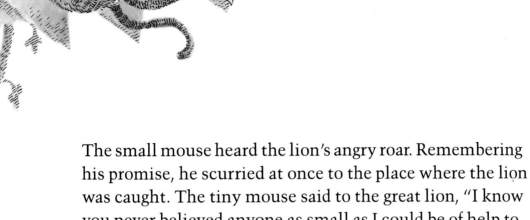

The small mouse heard the lion's angry roar. Remembering his promise, he scurried at once to the place where the lion was caught. The tiny mouse said to the great lion, "I know you never believed anyone as small as I could be of help to anyone as great as you. But now I will prove to you that it can be true."

With that, the mouse ran up the rope of the net. With his sharp, small teeth and his sharp, tiny claws, he chewed and tore a hole in the net just big enough for the mighty lion to wriggle through.

An act of kindness is never wasted.

The Wind and the Sun

One day the Wind and the Sun got into a fight. The Wind boasted that he was stronger than the Sun. The Sun insisted that he was stronger than the Wind. They fought for a day. They fought for a week. They fought for a month.

At last, to settle the matter once and for all, the Wind and the Sun agreed to have a contest. They decided that whichever one of them could make a shepherd take off his cloak would be the stronger.

The Wind was the first to try. He was sly. He thought he would simply blow the cloak away. So the Wind began to blow with all his fury. He made it hail. He tossed down snow.

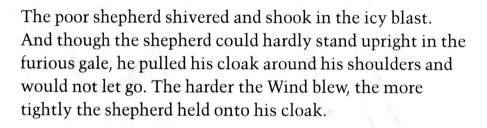

The poor shepherd shivered and shook in the icy blast.
And though the shepherd could hardly stand upright in the
furious gale, he pulled his cloak around his shoulders and
would not let go. The harder the Wind blew, the more
tightly the shepherd held onto his cloak.

At last, the Wind grew tired and could storm no more. He
vowed, "It cannot be done. That shepherd will never give
up his cloak."

The Sun just smiled. He shone down brightly and, with his warm golden rays, melted away the ice and snow from the Wind's bluster and blow.

Soon the shepherd grew warm. Then the shepherd felt hot. And, finally, the shepherd let his cloak drop to the ground.

Gentle persuasion is often more effective than violence.

The Dog and His Reflection

In the marketplace early one morning, a greedy dog snatched a tender, fresh steak from a butcher's wagon. "Stop, thief!" cried the butcher.

But the dog was too quick. He made off down the street with the meat clenched between his teeth. Running as fast as he could to the end of town, the dog came to a stream. A plank of wood was laid across it for a bridge.
"I will be safe in the woods on the other side to enjoy my meal in peace," thought the dog. And he started across the plank.

The stream was quite still. Not a ripple disturbed the surface of the water. Looking down, the dog saw his own reflection staring back at him.

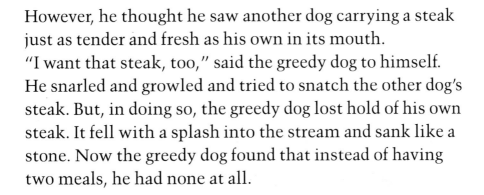

However, he thought he saw another dog carrying a steak just as tender and fresh as his own in its mouth.
"I want that steak, too," said the greedy dog to himself. He snarled and growled and tried to snatch the other dog's steak. But, in doing so, the greedy dog lost hold of his own steak. It fell with a splash into the stream and sank like a stone. Now the greedy dog found that instead of having two meals, he had none at all.

Be careful not to lose what you already have by being greedy for more.

The Hare and the Tortoise

On a country road, at midday, it happened that a hare who was going to town met a tortoise who was going to town. The fine, fast-footed hare said, "My goodness, Mr. Tortoise, you do move slowly. Your toes are so hooked and your legs are so small, it will be a wonder if you get to town at all."

But the plodding tortoise said, "Hooked or straight, small
or tall, I think I can beat you in a race to the town gate."
"Surely you are joking," said the hare.
"No, I am quite serious, Mr. Hare," replied the tortoise.
The arrogant hare laughed. He thought it was all so silly.
He said, "This will be fun. It will be the easiest race I've
ever won."

So the hare started off at a run, while the tortoise began in his slow, creeping crawl.

In no time at all, the hare was so far ahead of the tortoise that he thought he may as well stop to rest. He had a snack. He had a drink. Then the hare lay down, closed his eyes, and fell fast asleep in the shade.

TOWN 6 M

Meanwhile, the tortoise kept slowly plodding along on his hooked toes and small legs. He did not stop to snack. He did not stop to drink. And he certainly did not stop to wake the sleeping hare. He kept to his task. So, in time, the tortoise neared the town gate.

The hare continued to sleep. It was not until the setting sun's golden light tickled his whiskers that the hare finally woke up.

He knew it was late! And then he realized just *how* late, when he remembered his race with the slow-moving tortoise.

Gazing far, far down the road, the hare could barely make out the tortoise approaching the town gate. In an instant, the hare took off on his fine, fast feet, running faster than he had ever run before. How he strained to catch up with the tortoise!

But it was no use. The hare reached the town gate too late.
The tortoise had already won the race.

Slow and steady wins the race.

31

The Story of Aesop

The man we know as Aesop lived nearly 2,500 years ago in Greece. He was born a slave on the island of Phrygia. But, because of his cleverness and wisdom, his master freed him. From Phrygia, Aesop traveled to the court of King Croesus. There he used his fables to counsel the king and his noblemen on the ways of human nature.

Aesop's fables were much more than amusing stories. Each was created to illustrate a particular aspect of human character. Some fables warned people not to act in a certain way, while other fables simply showed how foolish people could be. And always, there was a moral at the end of each story that clearly stated the fable's purpose or lesson to be learned.

Aesop never wrote down any of his fables. He journeyed from place to place, reciting them in marketplaces and palaces. It was not until years after his death that someone thought to write them down and collect them together. Ever since, these morals have been passed on from generation to generation.

Aesop's fables are as accurate a dictionary of human nature today as they were when Aesop first spoke them.